Classic Pages

花衣吹笛人

[英]罗伯特·勃朗宁（Robert Browning）著
[英]凯特·格林威（Kate Greenaway）绘
孔谧 译

向凯特·格林威致敬

辽宁人民出版社

CONTENTS

I . HAMELIN Town's in Brunswick ················ 004

II . Rats! They fought the clogs and killed the cats ········ 006

III . At last the people in a body ················ 018

IV . An hour they sate in council ················ 022

V . "Come in!" the Mayor cried, looking bigger ········ 026

VI . And at the scarf's end hung a pipe ············ 028

VII . Into the street the Piper stept ············· 032

VIII . You should have heard the Hamelin people ········ 042

IX . A thousand guilders! The Mayor looked blue ······ 046

X . The Piper's face fell, and he cried ············ 050

XI . "How?" Cried the Mayor, "d'ye think I brook ······ 052

XII . Once more he stept into the street ············ 054

XIII . The Mayor was dumb, and the Council stood ······ 088

XIV . Alas, alas for Hamelin ················· 098

XV . So, Willy, let me and you be wipers ·········· 106

目录

一　不伦瑞克有个哈梅林镇 ································ 005

二　是老鼠！它们咬坏木屐，咬死了猫 ·················· 007

三　最终，人们聚集起来 ································· 019

四　市政会议开了一个小时 ······························ 023

五　"进来！"市长喊道，这下将来人看得更清楚 ······ 027

六　他的围脖尾端上悬挂着一支笛子 ··················· 029

七　于是，吹笛人走上街头 ······························ 033

八　你应该听到哈梅林人 ································· 043

九　1000盾！市长脸色发青 ······························ 047

十　笛手的脸色阴沉了下来，他喊道 ··················· 051

十一　"你想怎样？"市长叫道 ··························· 053

十二　吹笛手又一次走上了街 ···························· 055

十三　市长哑住了，幕僚呆住了 ························· 089

十四　哎呀，哈梅林镇的居民真悲哀 ··················· 099

十五　所以，小威利，权当我们是个消忆人吧 ········ 107

译后记 ·· 108

I.

HAMELIN Town's in Brunswick,

By famous Hanover City;

The river Weser, deep and wide,

Washes its wall on the southern side,

A pleasanter spot you never spied;

But, when begins my ditty,

Almost five hundred years ago,

To see the towns folk suffer so

From vermin, was a pity.

一

不伦瑞克有个哈梅林镇，
与著名的汉诺威市比邻；
威悉河水啊，又宽又深，
冲刷着城墙的南边；
这里是你不曾见过的美丽乡间；
可我要开讲的歌谣里，
故事发生在大约五百年前，
这里的人们深受害虫的折磨，
实在苦不堪言。

II.

Rats! They fought the clogs and killed the cats,

And bit the babies in the cradles,

二

是老鼠！它们咬坏木屐，咬死了猫，
　　还啃伤了摇篮里的小婴孩。

And ate the cheeses out of the vats,

啃遍了大箱子里的每块起司。

And licked the soup from the cook's own ladles.

舔遍了厨师汤勺里头的汤汁。

Split open the kegs of salted sprats,
And made nests inside men's Sunday hats.

把装咸鱼干的圆桶给咬破，
又在男人戴的礼帽里筑窝。

And even spoiled the women's chats,

甚至打断了女人们的闲聊，

By drowning their speaking

With shrieking and squeaking

In fifty different sharps and flats.

它们发出 50 种的升降调,
　　吱吱嘎嘎尖声叫;
　　让她们的谈话听不到。

III.

At last the people in a body
To the Town Hall came flocking:
"This clear," cried they, "our Mayor's a noddy,
"And as for our Corporation — shocking

三

最终，人们聚集起来

来到市政厅抗议：

"很显然，我们的市长是个蠢东西！

"我们的市政官员也笨兮兮。

"To think we buy gowns lined with ermine
"For dolts that can't or won't determine
"What's best to rid us of our vermin!
"You hope, because you're old and obese
"To find in the furry civic robe ease?
"Rouse up, sirs! Give your brains a racking
"To find the remedy we're lacking,
"Or, sure as fate, we'll send you packing!"
At this the Mayor and Corporation
Quaked with a mighty consternation.

"想想看,是我们给他们买了貂皮大衣,
"而那帮蠢货不愿也不能做出英明决策,
"成为帮我们消灭老鼠的官吏!
"或许你们希望老鼠横行四方,因为你们又老又胖。
"只会蜷缩在貂皮袍子里享乐,
"振作点吧,先生们!好好动动你们的脑袋瓜,
"找到急需补救的办法。
"不然,我们就把你们全都解雇!"
听了这话,市长和他的幕僚
颤抖着止不住。

IV.

An hour they sate in council,
At length the Mayor broke silence:
"For a guilder I'd my ermine gown sell;
"I wish I were a mile hence!
"It's easy to bid one rack one's brain —
"I'm sure my poor head aches again.
"I've scratched it so, and all in vain.
"Oh for a trap, a trap, a trap!"
Just as he said this, what should happen
At the chamber door but a gentle tap?
"Bless us," cried the Mayor, "what's that?"

四

市政会议开了一个小时。

最后,市长打破了沉默:

"为了保护这座城市,我愿意卖掉我的貂皮长袍;

"我多么希望我远离这场灾害。

"叫人绞尽脑汁是多么难办——

"我确信我可怜的头疼病又犯了。

"为了除害我彻夜不眠,却毫无办法。

"对了,快拿捕鼠夹,捕鼠夹,捕鼠夹!"

就在他说这句话的时候,看看发生了什么?

门外传来轻轻的敲击声?

"祝福我们吧,"市长喊道,"是谁在敲门?"

(With the Corporation as he sat,
Looking little though wondrous fat;
Nor brighter was his eye, nor moister
Than a too-long-opened oyster.
Save when at noon his paunch grew mutinous
For a plate of turtle green and glutinous.)
"Only a scraping of shoes on the mat?
"Anything like the sound of a rat
"Makes my heart go pit-a-pat!"

（市长和幕僚一起坐着，
他看起来既矮小又肥胖；
他的眼睛既灰暗又干涩，
像一只口子开得很长的牡蛎，
中午时分，他的胃口会大开，
能喝下一整盘绿油油浓稠的甲鱼汤。）
"只是鞋子在垫子上的刮擦声吗？
"要知道任何像老鼠的声音，
"都会让我的心怦怦直跳！"

V.

"Come in!" the Mayor cried, looking bigger:
And in did come the strangest figure!
His queer long coat from heel to head
Was half of yellow and half of red,
And he himself was tall and thin,
With sharp blue eyes, each like a pin,
And light loose hair, yet swarthy skin
No tuft on cheek nor beard on chin,
But lips where smiles went out and in;
There was no guessing his kith and kin,
And nobody could enough admire
The tall man and his quaint attire.
Quoth one: "it's as my great-grandsire.
"Starting up at the Trump of Doom's tone,
"Had walked this way from his painted tomb stone!"

五

"进来!"市长喊道,这下将来人看得更清楚:

一个打扮古怪的身影闪进门来!

来人从头到脚披了件长袍,

是件一半黄色、一半红色的长袍,

这人又瘦又高,

一双锐利的蓝眼睛,目光如炬,

头发稀疏,但皮肤黝黑,

脸颊上没有一点绒毛,下巴上更没有一根杂毛,

唇上却闪现着隐隐的笑意;

没人能说出他的身世,

也没人瞧得上,

身材高大、着装古怪的他。

有人说:"他长得像我的曾祖父。

"听这厄运之神的口气。

"这家伙是从那画好的墓碑里走来的吧!"

VI.

And at the scarf's end hung a pipe;
And his fingers they noticed were ever straying
As if impatient to be playing
Upon this pipe, as low it dangled
Over his vesture so old-fangled.

六

他的围脖尾端上悬挂着一支笛子；
人们注意到吹笛人的手指放在笛上，
不停地抚摸，仿佛等不及要吹响，
那笛子在他古老长袍旁低垂摆荡。

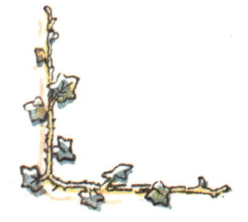

"Yet," said he, "poor Piper as I am,
"In Tartary I freed the Cham.
"Last June, from his huge swarms of gnats,
"I eased in Asia the Nizam
"Of a monstrous brood of vampyre-bats.
"And as for what your brain bewilders,
"If I can rid your town of rats,
"Will you give me a thousand guilders?"
"One? Fifty thousand!" Was the exclamation
Of the astonished Mayor and Corporation.

"而且,"他接着说,"别瞧不上像我这样穷的吹笛人。

"在鞑靼国,我用魔力让可汗如释重负,

"去年六月,助他赶走了蜇人的巨型怪物,

"又赶走了亚洲尼扎姆一窝可怕的吸血蝙蝠。

"让你们绞尽脑汁的鼠害,

"我也能帮你们解决掉!

"如果我把这座城的老鼠除光,

"你们会付我 1000 盾吗?"

市长和幕僚惊叹不已,承诺道:

"1000 盾?我给你 50000 盾!"

VII.

Into the street the Piper stept,

Smiling first a little smile,

As if he knew what magic slept

In his quiet pipe the while;

Then, like a musical adept,

To blow the pipe his lips he wrinkled,

And green and blue his sharp eyes twinkled,

Like a candle-flame where salt is sprinkled;

And ere three shrill notes the pipe uttered,

You heard as if an army muttered;

七

于是，吹笛人走上街头，

先是微微一笑，

仿佛他知道有种魔力在笛中沉睡；

接着他像音乐家一样，

噘着嘴唇，吹起笛。

他锐利的眼睛闪烁着宝石般的光芒，

就像撒了盐的烛火；

笛子发出了三声尖锐的音符，

听见了吗？那声音宛如千军万马的鸣啼；

And the muttering grew to a grumbling;
And the grumbling grew to a mighty rumbling;
And out of the houses the rats came tumbling.
Great rats, small rats, lean rats, brawny rats,
Brown rats, black rats, grey rats, tawny rats,
Grave old plodders, gay young friskers,

呜啼声渐渐变成了隆隆声；

隆隆声渐渐变成了轰鸣声；

老鼠们从四面八方的房子里翻滚出来。

大老鼠、小老鼠、瘦老鼠、胖老鼠，

褐老鼠、黑老鼠、灰老鼠、黄褐老鼠，

垂垂老矣的老鼠、快乐自在的小老鼠，

Fathers, mothers, uncles, cousins,
Cocking tails and pricking whiskers,
Families by tens and dozens,
Brothers, sisters, husbands, wives —
Followed the Piper for their lives.
From street to street he piped advancing,
And step for step they followed dancing,
Until they came to the river Weser
Wherein all plunged and perished!
Save one who, stout as Julius Caesar,
Swam across and lived to carry
To Rat-land home his commentary,

鼠爸爸、鼠妈妈、鼠叔叔、鼠堂兄妹，
翘着尾巴，支着胡须，
一大家子几十只老鼠，
鼠兄弟、鼠姐妹、鼠先生、鼠太太——
跟随吹笛人逃命。
从一条街到另一条街，吹笛人吹着笛子一步步前行，
老鼠们一步一步地跟着跳舞，
吹笛人将它们引到威悉河边，
老鼠们纷纷跳进了河里，全部淹死。
只有一只老鼠，像凯撒大帝一样强壮，
它游过了河，活了下来，
并将事情的经过带回到鼠国：

(As he, the manuscript he cherished.)
Which was, "at the first shrill notes of the pipe,
"I heard a sound as of scraping tripe,
"And putting apples, wondrous ripe,
"Into a rider-press's gripe,
"And a moving away of pickle-tub-boards,
"And a leaving a jar of conserve-cupboards,
"And a drawing the corks of train-oil-flasks,
"And a breaking the hoops of butter-casks;
"And it seemed as if a voice

（他心里谨记这次学到的教训：）
他说："那笛子发出的第一个尖锐的音符，
"我听到的是刮肚皮的声音，
"将非常成熟的苹果丢进榨汁机的搅动音，
"还有挪动腌菜桶盖板的动静，
"储藏室的门被打开了，
"鲸鱼油的瓶塞被拔开，黄油瓶子也被打烂，
"那听起来就像这些声音，

"(Sweeter far than by harp or by psaltery is breathed)
"Called out, 'oh rats, rejoice!
"'The world is grown to one vast drysaltery!
"'So munch on, crunch on, take your nuncheon,
"'Breakfast, supper, dinner, luncheon!'
"And just as a bulky sugar-puncheon,
"All ready staved, like a great sun shone
"Glorious scarce an inch before me,
"Just as me thought it said, 'Come, bore me!'
"I found the Weser rolling o'er me."

"(它们比竖琴或诗琴的声音美,)好像呼唤着我们:

"'哦,老鼠们,欢呼吧!

"'这世界是一个大宴厅!

"'所以,大吃大嚼吧,多好的美餐。

"'早餐、点心、晚餐和午餐!

"此时就像被打开的大糖罐,

"散发出太阳般的光!

"就像在我眼前不到一英尺的地方,

"我以为它在说:'来吧,跟我来吧!'

"而后便是威悉河的河水将我淹没。"

VIII.

You should have heard the Hamelin people
Ringing the bells till they rocked the steeple.
"Go," cried the Mayor, "and get long poles.
"Poke out the nests and block up the holes!

八

你应该听到哈梅林人
敲响了钟声,这声音甚至震动了尖塔。
"行动起来吧,"市长喊道,
"拿起长杆,
"捅破老鼠的巢穴,堵住它们的洞口!

"Consult with carpenters and builders,
"And leave in our town not even a trace
"Of the rats!" — When suddenly, up the face
Of the Piper perked in the market-place,
With a, "first, if you please, my thousand guilders!"

"在与木匠和建筑商咨询后,
"确信城里老鼠已经消失得无影无踪!"
突然间,吹笛人出现在集市。
他的面庞闪闪发亮,
说:"来吧,该是你们兑现承诺的时候了,
首先请支付我1000盾的报酬!"

IX.

A thousand guilders! The Mayor looked blue;

So did the Corporation too.

For council dinners made rare havoc

With Claret, Moselle, Vin-de-Grave, Hock;

And half the money would replenish

Their cellar's biggest butt with Rhenish.

To pay this sum to a wandering fellow

With a gipsy coat of red and yellow!

"Beside," quoth the Mayor with a knowing wink.

"Our business was done at the river's brink;

九

1000盾！市长脸色发青；

他的幕僚们也个个满脸的阴沉。

议会的晚宴上出现了罕见的混乱局面，

克莱特酒、摩泽尔酒、拉格拉夫酒、霍克酒；

酒窖里最大的酒桶里装着莱茵河酒，

所有这些只要500盾就能补充足够。

谁会把这么大一笔钱付给这个穿着红黄相间吉卜赛长衣的家伙！

一个闲逛的流浪汉！

"再说，"市长眨着眼睛说，

"我们的难事儿在河边已经办妥；

"We saw with our eyes the vermin sink,
"And what's dead can't come to life, I think.
"So, friend, we're not the folks to shrink
"From the duty of giving you something to drink,
"And a matter of money to put in your poke;
"But as for the guilders, what we spoke
"Of them, as you very well know, was in joke.
"Beside, our losses have made us thrifty.
"A thousand guilders! Come, take fifty!"

"我们都亲眼见证了老鼠被淹死、被除掉！
"相信我，那些老鼠不会再复活来骚扰我们的生活。
"所以，朋友，我们不是那种缩手缩脚的人，
"逃避给你兑现的承诺，
"出于礼节，我们邀请你一起来畅饮，
"我们也会把钱塞进你的口袋；
"但至于说到的 1000 盾，
"你很清楚，那就是个玩笑，
"而且，鼠害也让我们损失惨重，
"我们不得不节衣缩食，
"1000 盾！怎么可能，拜托，给你 50 盾已足够！"

X.

The Piper's face fell, and he cried,
"No trifling! I can't wait, beside!
"I've promised to visit by dinner-time
"Bagdad, and accept the prime
"Of the Head-Cook's pottage, all he's rich in,
"For having left, in the Caliph's kitchen,
"Of a nest of scorpions no survivor.
"With him I proved no bargain-driver.
"With you, don't think I'll bate a stiver!
"And folks who put me in a passion
"May find me pipe after another fashion."

十

笛手的脸色阴沉了下来,他喊道:

"别瞧不起我,啰里啰嗦!我等不及!

"我已经受邀去巴格达用晚膳,

"去喝首席主厨留在哈里发国王厨房的浓汤,

"那是他所有能拿得出手的东西,

"我让那儿的一窝蝎子无一幸存,

"这说明我不是个可以讨价还价的人!

"至于你,别以为我会吝啬对你的惩罚!

"还有你们这些让我愤怒的家伙,

"我会让你们见识我的笛子还有另一种魔力。"

XI.

"How?" Cried the Mayor, "d'ye think I brook
"Being worse treated than a Cook?
"Insulted by a lazy ribald
"With idle pipe and vesture piebald?
"You threaten us, fellow? Do your worst.
"Blow your pipe there till you burst!"

十一

"你想怎样?"市长叫道,

"你认为我可以受到比厨师长还差的待遇?

"被一个懒惰的无赖给侮辱?

"就凭你一支无用的笛子和破烂古怪的装束来羞辱?

"伙计,你是在威胁我们吗?那做好最坏的打算吧。

"随你怎么吹,即便把笛子吹爆掉,我们都无所谓!"

XII.

Once more he stept into the street,
And to his lips again
Laid his long pipe of smooth straight cane;

十二

吹笛手又一次走上了街,

将他的唇

又贴在光滑而笔直的长笛上;

And then he blew three notes

然后他吹了三个音符

(Such sweet

Soft notes as yet musician's cunning

Never gave the enraptured air)

（柔和的音符有着音乐家般的技巧，
　传递出令人陶醉的气息）

There was a rustling,

一阵沙沙声响，

that seemed like a bustling,

镇子一下子热闹起来，

Of merry crowds justling at pitching and hustling,

欢乐的人群似乎在推挤，在喧闹中奔走相告，

Small feet were pattering, wooden shoes clattering,

轻轻的脚步声啪嗒啪嗒,木鞋嗒嗒敲击着大地,

Little hands clapping and little tongues chattering,

孩子们拍着小手,小嘴叽叽喳喳,

And, like fowls in a farm-yard when barley is scattering,

而且，就像大麦散落时农场院子里一拥而上的家禽们，

Out came the children running.

All the little boys and girls,

那是镇子里所有的男孩儿和女孩儿,

With rosy cheeks and flaxen curls,

他们脸色红润,头发卷曲,

And sparkling eyes and teeth like pearls.

眼睛和牙齿像珍珠一样闪着光亮，

Tripping

他们绊倒了

and skipping,

再跳起来,

ran merrily after,

欢快地奔跑着，

The wonderful music with shouting and laughter.

美妙的音乐伴随着欢声笑语。

XIII.

The Mayor was dumb, and the Council stood
As if they were changed into blocks of wood,
Unable to move a step, or cry
To the children merrily skipping by.

十三

市长哑住了，幕僚呆住了，

好像变成一根根呆木头，

动也不能动，叫也不能叫，

眼看着孩子们又笑又跳地经过。

Could only follow with the eye
That joyous crowd at the Piper's back.
But how the Mayor was on the rack,
And the wretched Council's bosoms beat,
As the Piper turned from the High Street
To where the Weser rolled its waters
Right in the way of their sons and daughters!
However he turned from South to West,
And to Koppelberg Hill his steps addressed,
And after him the children pressed;
Great was the joy in every breast.
"He never can cross that mighty top!
"He's forced to let the piping drop,
"And we shall see our children stop!"

他们只能用目光追随着,
欢乐的孩子们跟在吹笛人的身后,
市长完全被架空。
可悲的幕僚们的胸脯激烈地起伏着。
当吹笛人从高街转身
到威悉河水滚滚的地方,
那是他们儿女必经的地方!
不过吹笛人却从南边转到西边,
他向科佩尔伯格山走去,
孩子们跟在他身后推来推去;
每个人心中都充满了喜悦:
"他永远无法越过那巨大的山顶!
"那会逼他停止吹奏!
"我们会看到孩子们停下来的!"

When, look, as they reached the mountain-side,

A wondrous portal opened wide,

As if a cavern was suddenly hollowed;

And the Piper advanced and the children followed,

And when all were in to the very last,

The door in the mountain-side shut fast.

Did I say, all? No! One was lame,

And could not dance the whole of the way;

And in after years, if you would blame

His sadness, he was used to say,

"It's dull in our town since my playmates left!

看啊！当他们快到达山腰时，
突然，半山腰奇妙地打开了扇大门，
瞬间一个山洞出现在眼前，
吹笛人走在前面，孩子们跟着进去，
当最后一个孩子走进山洞，
山腰上的大门瞬间关闭。
是所有人吗？不！还剩下了个瘸腿的孩子，
他一路上不能蹦蹦跳跳，
多年后，如果你责备他为何总是那么悲哀，
他会告诉你说：
"自从我的小伙伴们都离开后，
"我们的小镇就变得一蹶不振，

"I can't forget that I'm bereft
"Of all the pleasant sights they see,
"Which the Piper also promised me.
"For he led us, he said, to a joyous land,
"Joining the town and just at hand,

"我难以忘记,我失去了
"以前所拥有的快乐时光。
"吹笛人也答应过我,
"他说会带我们到一个欢乐国,
"去个新的镇子,而它好像就在眼前!

"Where waters gushed and fruit-trees grew,
"And flowers put forth a fairer hue,
"And everything was strange and new;
"The sparrows were brighter than peacocks here,
"And their dogs outran our fallow deer,
"And honey-bees had lost their stings,
"And horses were born with eagles' wings;
"And just as I became assured
"My lame foot would be speedily cured,
"The music stopped and I stood still,
"And found myself outside the hill,
"Left alone against my will;
"To go now limping as before,
"And never hear of that country more!'

"那里的清泉喷涌,果树常绿,
　"花朵绽放出一道道亮丽,
　"而每件事物新颖又稀奇;
"那里的麻雀都比这里的孔雀都缤纷靓丽,
　"那里的小狗比这里的小鹿都迅捷,
　　"那里的蜜蜂不再长毒刺,
　"就连马儿都长出老鹰般的羽翼。
"正当我确信他的诺言要实现,
　"我瘸的脚马上要被治愈,
"音乐突然止住,我却站在原地,
　"我发现自己被挡在山门之外,
"就剩下孤苦伶仃的自己,愿望没有实现。
　"只能像以前一样一瘸一拐,
　"再也听不到欢乐国里的消息!"

XIV.

Alas, alas for Hamelin!
There came into many a burgher's pate
A text which says that Heaven's gate
Opes to the rich at as easy rate
As the needle's eye takes a camel in!
The Mayor sent East, West, North, and South,
To offer the Piper, by word of mouth;
Wherever it was men's lot to find him,
Silver and gold to his heart's content,
If he'd only return the way he went,
And bring the children behind him.
But when they saw it was a lost endeavour,
And Piper and dancers were gone for ever.

十四

哎呀,哈梅林镇的居民真悲哀!
其实他们的心里都明明白白,
曾经有关于天堂之门的记载,
有钱的人想要进到那里去,
就像骆驼穿过针孔般不易!
市长曾经派人前往世界各地,
发出追捕令将吹笛人通缉,
市长承诺愿付给抓到者金银钱币,
开出的数目随抓到者的心意。
只希望吹笛人能够按原路返回,
将跟在他身后的孩子们一一带回。
但他们的努力毫无回报,
吹笛人和孩子们再也没返回。

They made a decree that lawyers never
Should think their records dated duly
If, after the day of the month and year,
These words did not as well appear,
"And so long after what happened here
"On the Twenty-second of July,
"Thirteen hundred and seventy-six."
And the better in memory to fix
The place of the children's last retreat,
They called it, the Pied Piper's Street—
Where any one playing on pipe or tabor,
Was sure for the future to lose his labour.

于是他们制定了一项新法令,
要求律师必须详实记录日期,
除了要记录某年某月某日,
还必须额外增添以下的文字:
"故事发生在很久以前,
"1376年的7月22日的那一天。"
为了牢记孩子们最后离开的地方,
人们将这里命名为"魔笛人街",
这里,任何一个吹笛子或敲鼓的人,
都无法找到工作、毫无前途,
也没有让他们可住的旅馆或酒馆,

Nor suffered they hostelry or tavern
To shock with mirth a street so solemn;
But opposite the place of the cavern
They wrote the story on a column,
And on the great church-window painted
The same, to make the world acquainted
How their children were stolen away;
And there it stands to this very day.
And I must not omit to say
That in Transylvania there's a tribe
Of alien people that ascribe
The outlandish ways and dress

供他们在如此庄严的街道上嬉笑喧闹,
在山腰洞口的对面竖立着告示柱,
人们将历史故事刻在上面,
并画在教堂的玻璃窗画上,
让全世界都知道这个故事,
知道他们的孩子是如何被拐走,
直到今天,柱子仍矗立在那儿,
我还要说的是:
在特兰西瓦尼亚,有个部落
都是外来的人,
生活方式和穿着都很荒唐,

On which their neighbours lay such stress,
To their fathers and mothers having risen
Out of some subterraneous prison
Into which they were trepanned
Long time ago in a mighty band
Out of Hamelin town in Brunswick land.
But how or why, they don't understand.

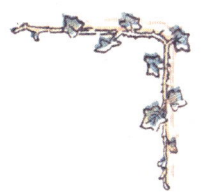

附近的人说，
他们的父亲和母亲是从某个地牢爬出，
在很久以前，他们受人引导，
从不伦瑞克的哈梅林镇跑来，
至于为什么会这样，他们也无从说起。

XV.

So, Willy, let me and you be wipers

Of scores out with all men — especially pipers!

And, whether they pipe us free from rats or from mice,

If we've promised them aught, let us keep our promise!

十五

所以，小威利，权当我们是个消忆人吧，

抹去对所有人的误解，尤其是吹笛人！

而且，不管他们是不是用笛子为我们消除了鼠害，

若我们曾向他们承诺过什么，请遵守诺言，去实现！

译后记

童心未泯的绘本创作者

凯特·格林威（Kate Greenaway，1846—1901），是英国19世纪最具影响力的童书插画家之一，甚至与创作《青蛙求偶记》（*A Frog He Would A-Wooing Go*）的蓝道夫·凯迪克（Randolph Caldecott）、绘制《睡美人》（*The Sleeping Beauty*）的沃尔特·克莱恩（Walter Crane）并称为"英国绘本三巨头"，他们三人大大地改变了现代图画书的表现形式，更引领了英国绘本的黄金发展时期。

凯特·格林威

成长于英国乡村的纯真之心

1846年，凯特·格林威出生于伦敦的雷克斯顿区（Hoxton）。因为父亲是一名绘图员和雕版印刷师，当格林威刚学会握笔的时候，父亲就鼓励她开始画画。稍长之后的格林威除了画画之外，也非常喜欢装饰自己的洋娃娃，小小年纪就展现出她对艺术的喜爱。12岁时，她进入皇家女子艺术学校（Royal Female School of Art）学习装饰艺术；之后就读于希瑟利艺术学校（Heatherley School of Fine Art），并在22岁时举办了她人生中的第一场水彩画展。

16岁的凯特·格林威

格林威在一个叫作罗雷斯顿（Rolleston）的小村庄度过了其童年的大段时光，她曾经说过："当我还是个孩子时，在乡间度过了非常快乐的时光。"乡村的老式英国风情和童年的愉快记忆对她的绘画风格产生了很大的影响，从她的作品中可以发现，画作里充满了浪漫的氛围，场景大多在田野、花园、牧场或是小村庄，笔下的人物则以女性和孩童为主。仔细评析格林威的画作可以发现，她强调细节，用色鲜明强烈，有其独特的纤细之美。

19世纪末的格林威风潮

19世纪70年代，英国有一位知名的木刻印刷师埃德蒙·埃文斯（Edmund Evans），他改善了彩色印刷的技术，大大提升了原本低劣的图画书品质，同时他也不断地挖掘优秀的插画家，并一同合作，共同出版图画书。格林威原本专为节庆贺卡绘制插图，埃文斯相中了她的风格，认为十分符合当时维多利亚时代的大众口味，便邀请她创作了格林威人生的第一本图画书——《窗下》(Under the Window)。

埃文斯曾说，当他一读完《窗下》的诗文和插图草稿之后，便深深为之着迷，于是他马上说服出版商出版此书，在首印时就大手笔地印了两万本，这在当时是相当庞大的印量。不过读者的反应证明了埃文斯的眼光没错，《窗下》果然大受欢迎，上市后便售罄，后足足加印了五万本。前前后后更再版多次，于格林威一生当中，总共销售超过十万本，相继翻译成德文、法文、日文等多国语言，着实成为了时代经典。

因为《窗下》在商业上的成功，插画中的人物穿着常被人拿

凯特·格林威的服装设计风格

来讨论研究。格林威笔下人物的服饰参照了18世纪末至19世纪初的穿着风格，虽然在格林威生活的19世纪末，这种风格被认为有些过时，但19世纪下半叶正处于欧洲的艺术服饰运动（Artistic Dress Movement），主张拒绝高度复杂僵硬的穿衣风格，兴起使用更为简洁的设计；同时也受到前拉斐尔派的艺术风格影响，让格林威笔下的服饰重新流行起来。因此，格林威成了一个家喻户晓的名字，甚至在当时掀起了一股格林威风潮（Greenaway Vogue）。

与同时期崭露头角的凯迪克即克莱恩相比较，格林威的作品从女性视角出发，风格较为细腻优美，她笔下的人物穿着18世纪后期流行的服饰，例如镶有花边的礼袍、头上和腰间都系着丝带；文字更多着眼于美好纯真的时光，关注孩子的天真烂漫、纯真朴实的心灵，与同时期的其他两位插画家的风格有着明显不同。

余音绕梁的经典

格林威大部分作品的文字都来自民间耳熟能详的歌谣，例如《鹅妈妈童谣》（Mother Goose）、《金盏花花园》（Marigold Garden）、《小安》（Little Ann）、《四月儿歌》（April Baby's Book of Tunes）、《儿童生日书》（Kate Greenaway's Birthday Book for Children）以及《苹果派》（Apple Pie）皆是以童谣改编而成。

1855年，为了纪念格林威对插画领域的贡献，英国图书馆协会（The Library Association）以她的名字创办了"凯特·格林威奖"（The CILIP Kate Greenaway Medal），此奖是英国历史最悠久并且最重要的绘本奖项，评选标准包含了艺术风格、格式、图文整合与视觉印象，对于插画的严格审视，让格林威奖在国际上有着极高的声誉，至今仍是许多插画家、作家角逐的绘本大奖。

无数英国孩子是在格林威插画的童书陪伴下长大的，有些甚至受到她的绘画风格影响，成为著名的插画家，如以花仙子系列作品（*Flower Fairies*）闻名的巴克（Cicely Mary Barker）就是其中一个例子。即使一百多年过去了，格林威的作品依然为全世界的读者喜爱着，每一次翻阅都能碰上可爱的孩子与风景，感受属于那个时代的艺术氛围，相信不论是大人或是孩子，都可以在这些经典图画书中获得美感和乐趣。

凯特·格林威故居，位于英国伦敦汉普斯特德，
由英国著名建筑师理查德·肖设计建造

消灭鼠患的吹笛人

本书《花衣吹笛人》（The Pied Piper of Hamelin）源自德国的古老民间故事，这则带有传奇色彩的故事最早可追溯到13世纪，几百年来，该故事也一直在全世界各地广为流传。过去，人们通过口耳相传的方式，逐渐发展出今日我们缩减的各种故事版本，在著名童话作者格林兄弟的《德国传说》中也有收录。

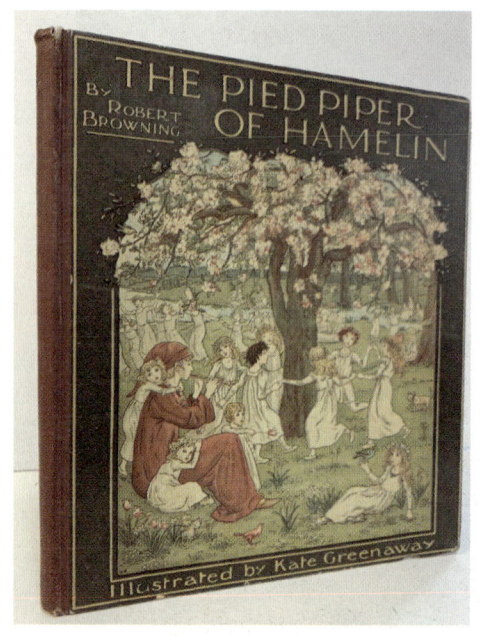 

虽然各版本的情节不尽相同，但故事大抵都围绕着一个叫作"哈梅林"的小镇，这里常年饱受鼠灾之苦，忍无可忍的居民群起

向市政厅抗议。这时，一个带着笛子、身穿花衣裳的神秘男人出现了，他对市长和市民说，只要给他1000盾，他就能施魔法将老鼠赶走。市长答应后，吹笛人便吹奏起他的笛子，老鼠们跟着笛声，竟然真的一只只跳入河中。可是解决鼠灾之后，市长及其幕僚竟然反悔，吹笛人一怒之下，再度吹起笛子，镇上的孩子们全都跟着吹笛人的脚步离开了城镇，从此再也没有回来。

故事中的哈梅林镇是个真实存在的地方，历史记载了当地在1248年发生了一起街头儿童失踪事件，从那之后，便衍生出许许多多传说，其中一个传说就是如今我们所知的《花衣吹笛人》。关

于这起事件的真实性众说纷纭,有学者认为故事中消失的孩子指的是13世纪到东欧殖民的年轻人,也有人认为是1212年的儿童十字军。因为传说故事的口述特性,今人已很难去考究故事的源流和真实性,不过这正是传说迷人之处,后世的作家可以借此传说,自由挥洒幻想之笔,去表现昔日各民族的所思所想。

19世纪,英国著名诗人罗伯特·勃朗宁(Robert Browning)为了安慰一位名叫威利的生病孩子,便将这则德国的民间传说写成英文版的儿童故事《花衣吹笛人》,搭配儿童插画家凯特·格林威精致细腻的插画,再度赋予这则古老传说新的生命。勃朗宁版本的《花衣吹笛人》充满韵律,他尤其擅长刻画人物的性格,如故事中官员们的形象、吹笛人的气质及民众的声音都好像离我们不远,读起来毫无陌生感。另外,老鼠们和孩子们奔跑上街的画面,也让读者读起来感到十分生动,仿佛耳边真的响起了笛声和奔忙的脚步声。

《花衣吹笛人》的结局虽像一团迷雾,但它的警世意味深长,故事最终提醒人们不该背信弃义,否则就会像哈梅林镇的居民一样遭受报复。尽管传说的情节通常有些夸大的成分,但不论故事到底是真实或杜撰的,情节本身的神秘气氛都深深吸引着世世代代的读者。

图书在版编目（CIP）数据

花衣吹笛人：英汉对照 /（英）罗伯特·勃朗宁（Robert Browning）著；（英）凯特·格林威（Kate Greenaway）绘；孔谧译. —沈阳：辽宁人民出版社，2024.7

（"世界儿童经典插图版"丛书）

ISBN 978-7-205-10829-8

Ⅰ.①花… Ⅱ.①罗… ②凯… ③孔… Ⅲ.①儿童故事—图画故事—英国—现代 Ⅳ.①I561.85

中国国家版本馆 CIP 数据核字（2023）第 156868 号

出版发行：辽宁人民出版社
地　址：沈阳市和平区十一纬路 25 号　邮编：110003
电　话：024-23284321（邮　购）　024-23284324（发行部）
传　真：024-23284191（发行部）　024-23284304（办公室）
http://www.lnpph.com.cn

印　　　刷：辽宁新华印务有限公司
幅面尺寸：180mm×210mm
印　　张：5
字　　数：55 千字
出版时间：2024 年 7 月第 1 版
印刷时间：2024 年 7 月第 1 次印刷
责任编辑：阎伟萍　孙　雯
装帧设计：留白文化
责任校对：冯　莹
书　　号：ISBN 978-7-205-10829-8
定　　价：57.00 元